THE LITTLE MERMAID

MOVIE CAMERA
Storybook with Film Viewer

Adapted by Judy Katschke and Olivia London
illustrated by Disney Storybook Artists

Reader's Digest Children's Books®

New York, New York • Montréal, Québec • Bath, United Kingdom

*M*any years ago the oceans and everything beneath were ruled by a powerful king named Triton. King Triton had seven daughters, and the youngest was Ariel. Ariel had everything a little mermaid could wish for. But Ariel longed to live above the sea like a human.

Almost every day, Ariel and her friends Flounder and Scuttle would visit the ocean

surface and watch the ships sailing in the distance. One day, Ariel and Scuttle swam up to a ship and peered through a porthole. Sitting on a barrel was a very handsome man.

The stranger was a prince named Eric. And in honor of Prince Eric's birthday his manservant, Grimsby, had just presented him with fireworks and a life-sized statue of himself. Suddenly, a loud clap of thunder interrupted the celebration. A hurricane was coming!

Ariel followed the ship as a bolt of lightning hit the deck, bursting it into flames. The ship crashed into a rock, throwing everyone overboard, including handsome Prince Eric!

Ariel quickly swam to the

drowning prince and dragged him unconscious from the water. She saved his life!

As Eric lay on the beach, Ariel sang to him. She hoped he would wake up and see her. The prince's eyes were shut, so he could not see Ariel, but he could hear her sweet singing voice. And he fell in love with her voice!

As Ariel watched over the prince, she had no idea that she was being watched by an evil sea witch named Ursula and her two eels, Flotsam and Jetsam. Ursula wanted to rule the ocean and defeat Ariel's father. Watching Ariel, she came up with an evil plan.

Later that day, Ariel swam with Flounder and another friend, Sebastian, to her grotto that held her souvenirs from the human world. She loved to sit in her grotto and dream

about the surface. But an angry King Triton soon appeared and blasted all of Ariel's treasures with his trident. He didn't want Ariel to have anything to do with the human world. He thought the human world was dangerous—too dangerous for his daughter.

In the grotto, Ariel sobbed. But she wasn't alone for long—Flotsam and Jetsam came by and told her that Ursula could make her dreams come true. Ariel had no idea what the eels meant, but she was desperate to meet Prince Eric. So Ariel swam with the eels to Ursula's lair while Sebastian and Flounder followed behind.

Ursula said she would make a potion that would turn Ariel into a human for three days. Before the sun set on the third day, she had to get Prince Eric to kiss her. If he did, Ariel would remain a human. If he didn't, she would turn back into a mermaid and belong to Ursula!

Ariel was about to sign the contract when Ursula told her what the payment would be— Ariel's voice!

Ariel didn't want to lose her voice, but she wanted to be with Eric. Seeing no alternative, she signed Ursula's contract and began to sing. Evil magic ripped the voice from her throat and passed it to Ursula.

Then Ariel's fins were transformed into two sturdy legs! She struggled to stay afloat, not knowing how to swim without her fins!

Sebastian and Flounder whisked Ariel up to the surface. They washed up in shallow water. Ariel stared at her new legs, and after a few wobbly steps she found herself running from Prince Eric's dog, Max!

The prince ran over to Max. When he saw Ariel his eyes lit up. Wasn't she the girl who saved him from drowning?

"What's your name?" Eric asked.

Ariel opened her mouth but no words came out.

Eric shook his head. The girl who saved him had a beautiful voice. But Eric invited Ariel and her friends to his castle! Ariel was given a bubble bath, then a dress to wear to dinner.

As she entered the dining room, Ariel was lovely. But then she sat down and began combing her hair with a fork!

Eric didn't mind. He thought his new guest was charming, even if she wasn't the girl he was searching for.

Place the Magical Moments cartridge into the camera to watch Ariel and Eric in the rowboat.

Magical Moments

The next day, Eric and Ariel strolled and danced their way through the kingdom. By evening they were rowing together on a peaceful lagoon.

All Eric needed was some encouragement to kiss Ariel. So Sebastian swam to the boat and sang a love song. Just as Eric leaned toward Ariel, ready to kiss her—CRASH—Flotsam and Jetsam plowed into the boat, tipping it over!

Ursula frowned as she watched the scene in her crystal bubble. She needed to get close to Prince Eric—immediately! Casting a spell, Ursula soon transformed herself into a beautiful human girl named Vanessa. She wore a magic necklace containing Ariel's voice.

Vanessa left her underwater lair for the prince's castle. She stood outside and began to sing, casting a spell of enchantment over Prince Eric. Almost at once, the prince chose to marry Vanessa! She had the voice of the girl who saved him.

The next morning, when Ariel heard the news, she was heartbroken. But as Vanessa gazed at her true reflection in her magic mirror, she knew everything was working perfectly. With no prince to kiss Ariel, Ursula had won!

Scuttle gasped as he secretly watched Vanessa. Flapping his wings, he flew to warn Ariel, Sebastian, and Flounder. The prince was marrying the sea witch in disguise!

Ariel and her friends had to stop the wedding! While Sebastian swam off to alert Triton, Scuttle rallied other seabirds and animals. They attacked Vanessa, breaking her magical necklace and her enchantment over Eric. As Eric came out of the spell, Ariel began singing with her own voice.

Eric smiled. Ariel was the girl he was looking for. But as he rushed to kiss Ariel, it was too late. The sun was setting and Ariel's legs turned into fins. As for Vanessa, she turned back into Ursula the sea witch!

"You're too late!" Ursula declared as she grabbed Ariel. Eric tried to rescue Ariel but he was no match for Ursula's powers.

Neither was King Triton as he tried blasting the sea witch with his trident. Finally, Ursula made the king a deal: Ariel in exchange for him!

To save his daughter, Triton signed Ursula's contract to give her control of the ocean. The sea witch cackled as she picked up the king's crown and trident that were hers at last. Then she tried to destroy Ariel!

But just as Ursula was about to destroy the mermaid with her new powers, Eric rammed the boat straight into her massive gut. The sea witch sank down into the sea.

The sea became calm. Ursula could no longer hurt Ariel or King Triton.

By the next morning, everything seemed to be back to normal. But as Ariel sat on her rock gazing out to shore, she was still in love with Prince Eric.

She couldn't forget the prince, even though they lived in two different worlds. She longed to be part of his world.

King Triton saw how sad Ariel was, and after a lot of thought, he knew what he had to do.

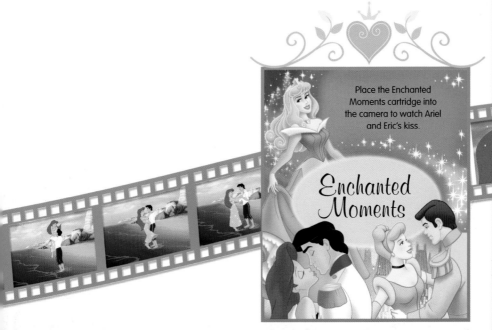

Place the Enchanted Moments cartridge into the camera to watch Ariel and Eric's kiss.

Enchanted Moments

With a wave of his trident, Triton turned Ariel's fins into human legs. Triton knew he would miss his daughter, but she had to be with her true love.

Ariel couldn't believe it! This meant she could be with Prince Eric in his world! The little mermaid ran into the arms of her handsome prince. Soon, Prince Eric would become Ariel's loving husband. And they lived happily ever after!